CHIPMUNK'S A B C

By ROBERTA MILLER
Illustrated by RICHARD SCARRY

A GOLDEN BOOK · NEW YORK

Copyright © 1963, renewed 1991 by Random House, Inc. All rights reserved. Originally published
in 1963 by Western Publishing Company, Inc. Published in the United States by Golden Books,
an imprint of Random House Children's Books, a division of Random House, Inc., New York.
GOLDEN BOOKS, A GOLDEN BOOK, A LITTLE GOLDEN BOOK, the G colophon, and the distinctive gold spine
are registered trademarks of Random House, Inc. A Little Golden Book Classic is a trademark
of Random House, Inc.
www.goldenbooks.com
www.randomhouse.com/kids
Educators and librarians, for a variety of teaching tools, visit us at
www.randomhouse.com/teachers
Library of Congress Control Number: 2005926654
ISBN: 978-0-307-02024-6
Printed in the United States of America
10 9 8 7 6 5 4
First Random House Edition 2007

A is for **apple tree**.

B is for **burrow**. Guess who lives in the **burrow** under the apple tree?

C is for **Chipmunk**. It is **Chipmunk** who lives in the burrow under the apple tree.

D is for **Donkey**. Chipmunk and **Donkey** have been out picking **daffodils**.

E is for **ears**. Chipmunk's mother
washes his **ears**.

F is for **friends**. Chipmunk has several
good **friends**. **Froggie** is a **friend**.

G is for **Goat**.

Goat plays a **game** with Chipmunk.

H is for **hide-and-seek**. Chipmunk and
his friends **hide** in **holes** and **hedges**.

I is for **ice cream**.

Donkey is serving **ice cream**.

J is for **jump**. Froggie **jumps** for **joy**.
He loves ice cream.

K is for **kitchen**. Chipmunk puts the **kettle** on. Mouse is slicing cheese with a **knife**.

L is for **lake**. Chipmunk and Bunny go sailing on the **lake**. Both wear **life** jackets.

M is for **mumps**. **Mouse** has **mumps**.
He listens to **music** and has **meals** in bed.

N is for **net**.
Chipmunk catches butterflies in his **net**.
Then he lets them go.

O is for **oboe**. Froggie plays the **oboe**.
Donkey drinks from an **orange** cup.

P is for **party**.

Chipmunk loves **parties**. Mouse is over
the mumps. He has brought Chipmunk a
present, a bunch of **pansies**.

Q is for **quilt**.
Chipmunk's mother is making a **quilt**.

R is for **river**, where Chipmunk and Donkey have a swimming **race**.

S is for **swing**.

Chipmunk likes to **swing** almost as much as he likes to **swim**.

T is for **telephone**.

Someone wants to **talk** to Chipmunk.

U is for **umbrella** to keep out the sun.

V is for **vacation**. Chipmunk is at the seashore, staying in a **villa** with a nice **view** of the sea.

W is for **wagon**. Goat pulls the **wagon**,
and Chipmunk rides. The **weather** is nice,
and they have a **watermelon** to eat.

X is a letter. Chipmunk and Bunny play
tic-tac-toe with an **X** and an O.

Y is for **yellow**. **Yellow** flowers grow in Chipmunk's **yard**.

Z is for **zipper**. Chipmunk **zips** his jacket.
He is going outside to play with his friends.